S...

OCCULT DETECTIVE

THE GRIMDITCH
BUTCHER

BRON JAMES

SAM HAIN
THE GRIMDITCH BUTCHER

PROLOGUE

That Wednesday had been just like any other for Douglas Norton. He had shut the shop at six o'clock, counted up the day's earnings, binned the produce that was no longer fit for sale, and then stopped for a couple of pints with the lads at *The Hog's Head* before heading home that night. This was a regular routine for him, and he would always take the same route home every night. It usually took no more than quarter of an hour, unless, of course, he needed to pick something up from the corner shop.

Tonight, Douglas didn't need anything from the corner shop, and he had started to make his way back home not long after nine o'clock. He turned left at the end of the road and into the gravel alleyway which ran along the back of a terrace of houses. It was the quickest route back home, leading around the back of the terrace, past the garage, and then down into the cul-de-sac where he lived. To one side of the narrow pathway stood the monotonous plain brick façade of the rear of the houses, the brickwork only occasionally broken up by graffiti or a downstairs-bathroom window; to the other side, suburban gardens hid behind tall wooden fences, and trees peeked their leafy heads over and reached down to any passers-by below. At either end of the path stood two lamp posts, but there were no other lights along the length of the alleyway, and the path was so long and winding that for the most part the road ahead was shrouded in darkness.

The gravel crunched noisily beneath Douglas's feet as he walked along. The night was a lot colder than it had been earlier that week, and Douglas briefly regretted not bringing a coat with him; the past few days had been unusually warm for January, but today, the weather decided it was still very much in the depths of winter. A chilling wind came blowing down the alleyway, and Douglas clutched his arms around himself to brace against the cold. It was then that he heard it.

It was not a noise he expected to hear down the often empty alleyway, and it was certainly not a noise he had heard before. It was like a low, guttural growl, a rumbling roar echoing off of the alley's walls. Douglas felt his body tremble with the noise, as if a low-flying aeroplane had just soared overhead, and then there was complete silence. An eerie stillness hung in the air. He turned around to see what on Earth could have produced such a sound, but he couldn't see anything. The alleyway behind him was dark and empty. Presuming it was just a weird effect caused by the wind blowing through the alley, or maybe the rumble of an oncoming storm, he turned around to carry on his way.

Without explanation, Douglas felt a sudden

and strange searing sensation pierce through his stomach, shortly followed by the feeling of something warm and wet. He looked down.

His white shirt being stained crimson red with blood was the last thing Douglas Norton ever saw.

CHAPTER I

The breakfast news was very rarely a source of good morning entertainment. On-going news stories would be briefly covered, broken up by smaller local news pieces, followed by several iterations of the weather and the ever pessimistic coverage of traffic on the M25. Alice watched the footage of motionless cars with very little interest as she chewed on a piece of slightly blackened toast. She only really had the television on to keep an eye on the time to make sure she wouldn't be late for work, but at least she now knew how long some people had been waiting in traffic whilst driving into central London, and she was particularly grateful not to be one of them.

'All right, I'm off,' Rachel announced as she walked through the living room, throwing on her jacket, 'I'll see you in a couple of days, I suppose.' She was going away on a mandatory two-day course of team-building exercises for work. Alice did not envy her.

'Have fun!' Alice chimed sarcastically. 'It won't be as bad as you think...'

The body of a man was discovered in an alleyway in Grimditch earlier this morning,' the newsreader announced, his voice just as flat and unmoving as his face, *'police on the scene of the murder are trying to piece together-'*

'A group of incredibly dull people for fake meetings, role-playing interviews, and getting teams to try to build bridges out of straws and tape. It's going to be an absolute riot,' Rachel retorted, rolling her eyes. 'How drinking-straw-architecture is in any way connected to customer service, I'll never know.'

'Look at it this way,' Alice said, swallowing the last bite of mildly burnt toast and standing up, 'it'll probably be better than working on the refunds desk for two days.'

'We'll see,' Rachel said doubtfully, and she hugged Alice goodbye, 'I'll see you on the other side.'

'See ya,' she said, and Rachel walked out of the front door, slinging her overnight-bag over her shoulder as she left.

'-is the third incident to have occurred this month.' The newsreader straightened himself, maintaining a cold and unblinking stare down the camera. *'Now here's Tom with the weather.'*

'It's looking grim, Jim,' announced Tom with the Weather, pointing to a map of London which had little cartoon clouds with sad faces on them.

Alice peered at the bottom-left side of the television screen to check the time. *07:13.* She gulped down the last of her cup of tea, and headed to the bathroom to quickly clean her teeth before having to leave. As much as she didn't envy

Rachel's team-building days, she also wasn't too enamoured with the idea of spending the next eight hours standing behind a till accepting a seemingly endless barrage of refunds and exchanges. She'd just started to clean her teeth when she heard a knock at the door.

'Fuhgut sum-thun?' Alice foamed through a mouthful of toothpaste as she pulled the door open, expecting to see Rachel there. However, standing in the doorway was not Rachel, but the familiar figure of Sam Hain, his greatcoat flowing down to his ankles and the rim of his fedora tilted over his eyes, clutching a crumpled newspaper beneath his arm.

'Have you seen the news?' He asked, holding up the paper and entering the flat. He glanced at the television, which was now recounting the story of a hamster who had climbed up a drainpipe, and – assuming this meant Alice had been paying attention to the rest of the news that morning – sat himself down on the sofa. 'Ah, excellent, you have. I won't need to fill you in then.'

'Wuh?' Alice frothed. 'Hol' on.' She darted off to the bathroom, spitting out the minty foam and quickly rinsing her mouth out before returning to the living room. She watched the news for a second to try to catch up with what Sam was saying. A hamster had climbed up a drainpipe and, despite having caused a blockage and survived a barrage of attempts to unblock it, had been reunited with its owner. 'Right, so what's got you interested in this story about a hamster?' She couldn't quite fathom the importance of a rodent in the drainpipe, but from what she'd come to know of Sam Hain, anything was possible.

'No no no,' Sam said, unfurling the newspaper in front of him, 'nothing to do with hamsters. This.' He pointed a finger at a news article, a page-long piece about a recent string of murders in the east end, headlined with the tasteful title *The Grimditch Butcher*. 'You haven't been following this then?'

Alice shook her head. 'Nope. And?' She didn't much care for sensationalist news coverage of murder victims.

'And? And what?! Three dead, all in similar circumstances, in the past month! And one of them was found in the early hours of this morning.'

'Why am I not surprised you get excited about murder?'

'It's not the murder itself, it's this.' Sam took out a sheet of folded paper from his inside pocket, and laid it out in front of Alice. Printed on it were pictures of the previous two murder cases, the bodies of the victims prominently displayed in the centre of each image. In each case, the bodies were laying on their backs, limbs sprawled out and their clothes stained red around the abdomen, a pool of blood coagulating around them. Any police involvement had mostly been cropped out of the images, so each one focussed largely on the bloody corpse, although the occasional elbow or hand still found its way into shot.

'Elliot Ferguson, a candlestick maker, and

Brian Mayweather, a pastry chef, were both found dead within these past few weeks, both in similar circumstances. And now, there's been a third.' Sam detailed, indicating to the bodies pictured.

'Wait, hold on. Did you say "candlestick maker"?' Alice asked.

'Well, yes. Elliot Ferguson was a candlestick maker.'

'Is that even a real profession? Aren't candlesticks made in factories now we're not living in the middle ages?'

'Well, yes, I suppose so, but that's not the interesting point! What links these victims?' Sam said, pointing to the pictures again.

'They were stabbed in the stomach...'

'Yes, and...?' Sam asked, gesturing as if trying to lead Alice to the answer.

'There's obviously something weird about it, otherwise you wouldn't be looking at me like that.' Alice looked back at the pictures, but didn't say anything more about them.

'No? Okay then, see the stab wounds, here and here,' Sam pointed, 'do you notice anything about them?'

'They're like patterns.'

'Yes, but, these aren't just any patterns,' Sam sounded far too enthusiastic for someone who was looking at pictures of formerly-living people. He pointed at the patterned wounds again. 'These symbols, they look like sigils. They're symbols of power, used for evoking and manifesting a spellcaster's intent.'

'What intent?'

'That depends on the one who is casting them. They can be invoked to do anything, from making it rain and boosting lottery chances, to inflicting pain and summoning demons. Very powerful magick in the right – or wrong – hands. And these people... Well, these aren't just your run-of-the-mill murders, and they're certainly not a part of a ritual spell to attract health and prosperity. This is blood magick.'

Alice stared at the images for a while longer before looking back up at Sam. 'And you're thinking we should go and investigate a murder which is more than likely linked to powerful, sacrificial blood magick rituals?'

'Absolutely,' was his simple reply.

'To be fair, I don't even know why I had to ask,' Alice said, looking for her shoes. 'So what do these sigils mean?'

'I have no idea,' Sam said frankly, 'but I have a plan to find out.'

'What's the plan?'

Sam stood up, straightening the lapels of his coat. 'We'll take a cab to Grimditch, we'll be there in about quarter of an hour. The magickal footprint of this will still be fresh, we'll be able to sense any disturbance in the Akasha. With any luck, the coroner won't have moved the body to the morgue yet, and I can get a proper look at the carvings in the latest victim.'

'Yes, with any *luck*...' Alice said, pulling on her boots. She wasn't particularly enthusiastic about the idea of starting her day with a corpse, but she couldn't deny she was interested in seeing it from Sam's unique point of view. There was something almost exciting about a magickal murder, although Alice was sure she'd probably change her mind quite quickly when face-to-face with the reality of it. She double-knotted her laces and stood up.

'All right then, let's go,' Sam said, making his way out of the door. Alice started to follow.

'Wait. You may want to lose the hat at least before we go anywhere,' she said.

'Why?'

'You want to go to a crime scene, and you're dressed like you're on your way to a fancy dress party as a film noir detective. If you were any paler, you'd actually be in black and white.'

Sam stood still for a moment, contemplating her suggestion. 'The hat stays,' he announced, as if coming to an important conclusion, and marched off down the corridor and towards the stairs.

The black cab drove smoothly down Islington high street. The traffic seemed to be surprisingly light for that time of the morning, and the taxi driver had mostly kept himself to himself, not really engaging in small-talk with either of his passengers. Sam appreciated both of these things.

'Bollocks!' Alice suddenly exclaimed, causing the taxi driver to jump slightly in his seat.

'What's the "bollocks"-ing for?' Sam asked, still gazing vacantly out of the taxi's window.

'I'm meant to be at work in ten minutes,' she said, pulling her phone out of her pocket. They'd just driven past the Angel underground station, which – had she have been going to work-work rather than off on some supernatural-murder-mystery-work – Alice should have been boarding the tube at right that very moment. She tapped at her phone's screen, coughing and making a strange wheezing noise. 'How do I sound?' She croaked, suddenly sounding as if she were on her deathbed.

'Like you're dying of a horrible debilitating virus,' Sam replied bluntly. He could hear the muffled ringing of the phone, shortly followed by the clicking of someone the other end picking up the receiver. Alice thrust a finger up in front of her pursed lips, staring at Sam, and she put the phone up to her ear.

'Hey,' her voice creaked like the floorboards of a dilapidated old Victorian town-house, 'I'm so sorry about this, but I'm afraid I won't be able to make it in to work this morning.' She coughed violently down the phone to drive home her point. It was a miracle she didn't force a lung up in the process. 'I'll take some flu medicine or something, and I should be able to come in this afternoon if you set my shift back a bit?' She followed this with a sniff and a half-hearted splutter.

'God no, you sound dreadful,' came a voice from the phone, *'just rest-up and get better, okay. Liz can*

'Oh, thank you so much,' she wheezed, 'I'll see you Monday.' She hung up, but not before choking out a few extra coughs away from the phone for added authenticity. 'There, that's that,' Alice announced with her usual cheery and not-at-all-flu-y voice, and put the phone back in her pocket.

'You are a woman of many talents, Miss Carroll,' Sam said with a subtle smile.

The taxi driver rolled his eyes. *Oldest trick in the book,* thought he.

Grimditch was an unusual place. It was a small region in the east end of London, but despite being a part of the city it felt more like a village or hamlet; just without any surrounding countryside, and with a strip club immediately next door to a fast food establishment. There was a single high street, populated by a few corner shops, a butcher's, a pharmacy, and a generous amount of run-down looking pubs and nightclubs. This street then linked to the surrounding housing estates, and just beyond those stood several bland, towering blocks of flats, looming like concrete giants over the district below.

Sam and Alice exited the taxi a short distance from the alleyway where the body had reportedly been found, and started to make their way towards the scene of the murder. Alice's first impressions of the place were hardly positive; it didn't help that the weather had forgotten about the early Spring it had been promising, and instead decided it was going to be cold and overcast. Large, grey clouds hung low over Grimditch, and a bitter wind swept through the streets. At least the place was living up to its name.

As they approached the alleyway, Sam quickened his pace to a purposeful stride, marching with conviction up the gravel pathway, his coat swishing back and forth rhythmically. Alice jogged a little to catch up, and matched his pace. The alleyway was an enclosed space, Alice thought, with the houses towering over her on the left, and gnarled trees leaning over the fences to her right. She wouldn't feel comfortable if she had to walk down this alley on her own. Doubly so now that someone had been murdered there.

Ahead of the two of them, a small congregation of police officers were gathered around a cordoned off area of the pathway. Behind the cordon stood a large white tent, completely concealing the site where the body had been found. Sam cut a confident swagger over to the police, making sure he was a few paces ahead of Alice. As he drew closer to the cordon, a sergeant stepped forward, holding his hand out to stop them from going any further.

'Sir, madam, I'm going to have to a-' the sergeant started, but Sam quickly cut him off.

'Arthur Doyle, consulting detective,' he said with an authoritative tone and a quick wave of what Alice presumed was a fake police ID, 'and this is my colleague.' Sam gestured in Alice's direction.

'Joan... Joan Wilson,' Alice offered hesitantly, stepping forward and extending her hand to shake that of the police sergeant. He simply stared back at her, ignoring her out-stretched hand.

'We were dispatched to aid in the investigation,' Sam concluded, and attempted to push past the sergeant.

''scuse me, sir,' the sergeant said, placing a firm hand on Sam's chest, holding him in place, 'we have everything under control here. May I ask who sent you?'

Alice could see the cogs whirring in Sam's head as he tried to come up with a convincing cover.

'Anderson. Homicide desk,' he said determinedly. He didn't have a clue if Anderson was a real person or not, nor – if he was indeed real – whether or not he worked on the homicide desk. It was a gamble, but Sam often found that if he said things with enough confidence and authority then people tended to believe him.

There was an unnaturally long pause, and Sam was starting to feel nervous. Maybe the sergeant knew Anderson. Maybe the sergeant *was* Anderson. Maybe there wasn't even an Anderson, and this man knew it! He tried to maintain his authoritative composure whilst he waited for what felt like an eternity for the sergeant to pass his judgement.

'All right then, go on through,' said the sergeant with a nod, and he waved Sam and Alice on through.

'Thank you, sergeant,' Sam replied, making his

way past the cordon, lifting the "Police Line Do Not Cross" tape over his head as he ducked beneath it, and walked towards the tent. He breathed a sigh of relief.

'You do realise that impersonating an officer of the law is a criminal offence, don't you?' Alice hissed at him when she was sure they were not in earshot.

'Trust me, this isn't the first time I've bluffed my way through something. I know what I'm doing.' It was true, he had bluffed his way through things before, but stating he knew what he was doing may have been a bit of an exaggeration.

'I'm sure. Is that how you got your hands on a fake police ID?'

'When you've seen a few IDs, you can replicate one to a passable standard, provided they don't look at it for too long. Comes in handy with freelance detective work,' he replied, nodding in greeting to one of the guards posted outside of the tent, and pushed his way through the entrance.

The scene inside had been carefully preserved for further investigation, with a small number of little yellow placards placed around key details. The gravel path had been kicked and scuffed around, with signs of disturbance – presumably caused by the dragging of feet – leading away from the middle of the path and towards the grassy verge. The blades of grass were stained a deep, rusty red, painted as if with a single oily brush-stroke in one particular direction. Towards the body itself.

It was a surreal sight, seeing this thing which had once been a person now laying sprawled out by the side of the path like an old discarded rag-doll. The legs were positioned not unlike that of the figure on a wet floor sign, with the arms also spread in a weird, angular way. In the middle of the victim's white shirt was a large rip, surrounded by a crimson-red stain. The collar and shoulders were also stained with blood, and red flecks marred the sleeves of the shirt, but that was where the body of evidence ended. Where one would normally expect to see a neck and head, there was nothing but a bloodied stump.

Alice turned away from the sight, feeling her stomach churning more and more with every second she spent staring at the headless body. Instead, she knelt down by a leather wallet, marked with a yellow placard numbered "2", and pretended to examine it with great interest. An uncomfortable lump formed in her throat, but she swallowed it and tried not to think about it too much.

Sam made his way over to the officer who was stood over the body, picking up a pair of rubber gloves from the nearby table as he went. 'What's the situation?'

'You the DI?' The officer asked, straightening himself up as Sam approached.

'I am.'

'What's with the get-up?' He looked Sam up and down with a sceptical expression.

'What do you mean?'

'You just look like what my son would dress up as if he was going to a Halloween party as a detective, that's all. Would've thought you'd want to wear one of the regulation jump-suits or something. Anyway...' The officer turned his attention to the headless body. 'One victim, found earlier this morning, deceased for around maybe ten or twelve hours. Was found on this verge, partially concealed by a pile of leaves,' the officer reeled off as if reading from a shopping list. 'Victim was found headless, and with a substantial abdominal wound. There's no evidence of much of a struggle. A bloody hand-print was found on the wall next to the body, presumably where the victim attempted to regain his balance before...' He trailed off, and ran his index finger across his neck, miming decapitation. Sam didn't really understand why the amateur dramatics was somehow better than saying 'beheaded.'

Alice tried to conceal her revulsion as she listened in on the description, and tried to distract herself by focussing on the wallet and its contents. She felt distinctly uncomfortable about the whole situation; not only was she a few feet away from a headless body, but she was also now rummaging through its wallet. She flicked through the collection of credit cards and café loyalty cards, and she peered into the change pocket; amongst the standard loose change were a couple of crumpled old receipts, some commemorative coins, a token with a golden logo on the front, and a half-torn lottery ticket. Nothing of any interest.

Sam grimaced as he looked down at the body.

'ID?'

'Hard to get a positive ID without a head 'n' all, but according to the driver's license and credit card in his wallet: Douglas Norton, forty-two years of age. We're now awaiting clearance to search his residence and workplace.'

Sam nodded. He looked down at the body with a morbid fascination, and his eyes traced the trail of scuffed gravel and the occasional streak of blood back towards the middle of the path. From what he could tell, the body had been dragged at least eight feet from its initial position.

'Looks like the victim was initially injured here,' Sam said, stepping back towards the point where the scuff marks came to an end. There was a small pool of dried blood at his feet, leading off onto a trail which grew heavier and heavier until it joined the body. 'There's significantly less blood here, probably from the initial stab-wound. Presumably these marks are from where the victim was dragged, and then decapitated here.' He walked back over to the body and knelt down by the side of it, pulling the pair of rubber gloves on with a snapping sound. 'If I had to hazard a guess, I'd say that the murder weapon wasn't removed from the man's abdomen until he had been dragged back to this spot here.'

What the hell am I doing here? Alice thought to herself. She didn't have the stomach for bloody beheaded corpses, or any blood for that matter. She had enough difficulty watching hospital-based soap operas (although admittedly the state of the patients weren't always the worst things about those series).

Poring over the body, Sam gently pried away the torn and tattered fragments of shirt from around the stab-wound. The cotton was crusty with dried blood, and required some convincing to come unstuck from the browning congealed tear in the stomach, but Sam could start to see that his suspicions were right. 'Al-... Joan, could you come and look at this please?'

It took a few seconds for Alice to realise he was actually talking to her, and a few seconds more to try to find a way of not looking at the dead body. 'I'd rather not...' *Please don't make me. Please don't make me. Please don't make me.* 'I'm, uh, busy over here.' She flapped the wallet about a bit.

'It's important,' Sam said, peering at her over his shoulder.

Bugger. She stood up from her rigorous inspection of the wallet and tentatively made her way towards him. And Douglas Norton. The headless, bloody body of Douglas Norton.

'Note the pattern of the abdominal wound,' Sam said, pointing to one of the many things in the vicinity of the one place Alice was trying her best not to look. Still, she looked to where he was pointing. The wound was not just any wound. A large bloody hole, presumably the entry wound, was where the belly button would have been on a non-cut-up person, and from there the pattern cut into the flesh spiralled outwards, forming a grotesque and unearthly symbol. The symbol twisted and turned at strange angles and seemed to be surrounded by other smaller symbols, but Alice had to look away before she could even begin to make sense of its shape. She swallowed heavily.

'Like the others?' She asked in a hushed tone, and Sam nodded morosely.

'You mean the other cases this month?' The officer enquired, standing behind them and peering over their shoulders. 'It does bear some similarities with the others. This is the first headless one, though.'

'Any sign of the murder weapon?' Sam asked, standing up. As he turned to face the officer, he slipped the transphasic energy probe into Alice's hand. She felt the cold metal of the TechnoWand in her palm and held on to it. As she clasped it, she thought she felt it vibrate in response.

'No, I'm afraid not. Same with the previous cases, too,' the officer explained, 'the killer may not have hidden the bodies well, but aside from that the scenes have been clean. No prints, no weapon, no evidence of any kind other than the body itself. All we have to go on are these strange patterns. My guess is that our killer likes scaring people, so he leaves the bodies in plain sight with a little signature to sign his work, but still cleans up anything which might lead us to him.'

While the officer was distracted with Sam, Alice slowly moved the probe over the body. She assumed that was what Sam had wanted her to do, anyway. She watched what she was doing out of the corner of her eye, squinting with disgust and trying her best not to think of the fact that her hand was now no more than a few inches away from a beheaded corpse. It seemed to be working, though, as the crystal at the probe's tip glowed intermittently, accompanied with a dull vibration through its metal body. *Definitely something out of the ordinary here then...*

The officer's radio started to blare a static crackling noise, and a voice almost entirely indiscernible shouted something through it. The voice mumbled and crackled its way through a garbled sentence, and the officer nodded. Police officers have a unique ability to make sense of garbled communications which no-one else can understand. Second only to train conductors. 'Copy that,' the officer stated, and turned to face Sam. 'You'll want to start making your way back to the high street, we've got a warrant to search the victim's workplace.'

'Where are we heading?' Sam asked.

'The butcher's shop,' replied the officer, and spoke into his radio again. 'I'm sending *Sam Spade* your way.'

Maybe I am a bit too film noir... Sam thought as he and Alice were led towards one of the police cars. Alice handed the probe back to Sam and gave him a subtle nod.

Standing outside of the butcher's shop, Sam and Alice stared at the scene which lay before them, dumbfounded. Alice stood in silence, her mouth slightly hanging open in shock. She turned away from the sight, retching. The police had only just opened up the front of the shop, revealing the horrific image it had been hiding.

There, sitting prominently in the middle window of the butcher's shop, surrounded by hanging porcine carcasses and select cuts of beef, sat the severed head of Douglas Norton, his mouth a-gape and a shiny red apple clasped between his teeth. His eyes were wide-open, but were partially concealed by a pair of novelty sunglasses, and a Hawaiian-style sun-hat rested upon his head. A wreath of fake pink flowers were wrapped around what had once been Douglas Norton's neck.

'Well, at least that solves the mystery of the missing head,' Sam said.

CHAPTER II

The smell of meat hung heavily in the air of the butcher's shop, as if the stench of death was clinging to every surface. It wasn't a pleasant aroma by any means, made all the worse by the knowledge that the severed head of a man now sat in the window. Alice had elected to stay outside for a while to catch some air, at least until the head had been removed from the scene, whilst Sam jumped straight on in to carry on with his investigation.

It was fairly standard in terms of butcher's shops; animal bodies hung down from the ceiling on meat hooks, morbid displays of body parts decorated the window, and a selection of complementary sauces lined the shelves on the back wall. Sam found the whole thing repellent; exactly why people still wanted to eat the meat after shopping here was beyond him. Through the door towards the back of the shop was a large walk-in freezer, filled with frozen goods and the rather haunting image of rows and rows of pig carcasses. But nothing seemed to be out of place, broken or disturbed in any way. Aside from the human head which now decorated the shop front, it was a perfectly normal butcher's shop.

'Looks like we have ourselves a phantom,' one of the officers remarked idly as he peered around the shop, taking down a few notes in his pad.

'Pardon?' Sam said, suddenly looking up from where he'd been staring at the severed head. He was more than a little surprised; he wasn't really expecting the Metropolitan Police to consider something supernatural.

'Phantom suspect,' the officer replied. 'No witnesses, no murder weapon, no evidence of a break in... No evidence of any kind. We've not got much to work with. Whoever did this was able to make themselves vanish, leaving no evidence other than those sick symbols.'

'Ah,' Sam replied, a little disappointed that he hadn't found a new associate with access to actual search warrants. He carried on examining the severed head, taking great care to not touch it.

The head of Douglas Norton was ghostly pale and his eyes were glazed over, as if staring into a void beyond the veil of reality. It was a haunting sight to behold. Sam had had very little experience with dead bodies, even less so with decapitated heads, and he was starting to regret wanting to be on a case involving a proper murder. It always seemed like an exciting prospect to him, but now he was actually investigating one he wasn't enjoying it quite as much as he'd thought he would. *Reanimated corpses, yeah,* he thought, *the undead risen? Of course, not a problem! But an actual dead-dead person...? Blimey.* Supernatural cases were often exciting and intriguing, sometimes even fun, but now that human lives were clearly at stake...

Working out murder cases by piecing together the evidence supplied by the news had been a hobby for him, but that and having the severed head of a murder victim actually in front of him were two completely different things. He shook that thought from his mind as he tried to focus back on Douglas Norton's head.

It didn't really betray any marks of the paranormal, although he wasn't too sure what he had been expecting. It was eerie and off-putting, but aside from that he wasn't really coming to many other conclusions. The most he could say was that yes, this head had at one point been connected with the body in the alleyway, and as far as he was concerned there was something more to this than met the eye (in his line of work, wasn't there always?). Whatever that something more was would have to wait, however, as the officer was now approaching him with an expectant look on his face.

'So what's the verdict, detective?'

Sam swallowed quite audibly as he tried to think of a quick and passable answer. 'Well, uh, as you can see,' he started, and pulled back the wreath of fake flowers wrapped around what had been Douglas Norton's neck, 'the head was severed along here.' He pointed to the very evident place where the neck ended and the body promptly failed to begin. The officer nodded.

'Hmmhmm. I can see that.' The officer was

clearly unimpressed with his deduction, and gestured for Sam to continue.

'To be honest, officer, it's too early to say anything conclusively,' he said, 'as you said, whoever did this knew how to cover their tracks. This joint is clean.' *This joint is clean,'* Sam thought to himself, *maybe try not to borrow too many clichés from crime dramas...* 'You know, severed heads not withstanding,' he added, looking back at the head. 'Maybe the coroner might have more luck inspecting the victim and his, uh, dislocated head?'

'Okay, we'll have the head dispatched to join the rest of the victim,' replied the officer, signalling to another to come over and collect the head. It was hastily placed inside a cooler and carried outside to a nondescript black van, which had just pulled up outside.

'Now that's interesting...' Sam mused as something out of the ordinary caught his eye. Where the head of Douglas Norton had been sat was a bloody mark. It wasn't simply a matter of the blood from the severed head leaking onto the surface and drying there, it was far too precise for anything like that. It was a spiral shape, radiating anti-clockwise and drawn in blood, with five smaller shapes – sigils – dotted around the outside of the spiral. It was more than a little reminiscent of what had been carved into the Void crystal found during the night in Knightsbridge.

'Please send my colleague in, officer,' Sam said, peering closely at this new revelation. As the officer walked away to call in Alice, Sam whipped out the transphasic probe and quickly waved it over the blood stain. The crystal turned a shade he could only describe as purple-black. It couldn't really be said to have glowed, as the colour it turned seemed more like an absence of light than anything else. He raised a curious eyebrow as he examined the weird, shadowy aura the crystal was now generating.

'Has the head gone yet?' Alice asked as she was led in by the officer, slightly averting her eyes and prepared to suddenly cover them just in case she saw a body-part which really should have been attached to a body. Sam quickly pocketed the probe, and beckoned for Alice to come over.

'It's fine, the head's on its way to the coroner. I just wanted you to have a look at this,' he said, pointing down at the bloody spiral. As Alice approached, she could see why he'd called her in.

'That's what I think it is, isn't it?' She asked, knowing full well the answer.

'I'm afraid so,' Sam said with a nod, 'and thank you, officer...?'

'Smith. Officer Smith,' replied Officer Smith.

'Thank you, Officer Smith. Oh, also, get the rest of forensics in here. We're going to need to dust for prints.' After years of watching crime dramas, he'd always wanted to say that sentence.

'I'll have a team sent in ASAP.'

As Officer Smith walked away, Sam turned back towards the spiral and sigils. He stared at it silently for a long time, lost in thought, before turning his attention to Alice. 'Alice, listen, I very rarely say this... Actually, I can't remember the last time I had to,' his voice was uncertain and concerned, 'but you're going to have to leave.'

'What?' Alice asked, taken aback. 'Is it because I couldn't stand to be in the same room as that severed head? Because I think that's a perfectly normal reaction to have to severed heads.'

'No, it's nothing to do with that. What we're facing is... Look, human lives are at risk, and I really don't know what to expect next. If this means what I think it means,' he said, pointing to the sigils, 'then it's connected to the oncoming darkness. Whatever was behind the Void portal, and everything that happened to you on Halloween, I don't know what or why, but...' He sighed. 'I don't want to put you in any unnecessary danger on this case.'

She looked deep into his eyes, and could feel his concern. She'd never really thought about him being emotionally vulnerable, but in this instance she could see and feel his worry, even if she didn't share his concern for her safety. 'What, and you think that I'm just going to leave you to it? I've come this far, I may as well stay with you and see this through to the end,' she said, 'besides, if it is connected with that thing that ended up inside my head, then I'd like to give it a piece of my mind! Figuratively speaking.' She could see Sam wasn't particularly happy with that idea. 'Okay, the minute things look like they could be taking a turn for the worse, I promise I'll get out of the way.'

Sam nodded begrudgingly. 'Good,' he said, although he didn't seem to mean it, 'I told you when we first met that it's not all quite as fantastical and magical as people might think, but I never thought you'd have to witness something like...' He held her by the shoulders for a moment, but soon released them, swallowing his anxiety and clapping his hands together. 'Anyway!' He span around, looking around the butcher's shop.

'What are you thinking?' Alice asked, trying to get back in on the case. Now that the head of Douglas Norton had gone, and there wasn't a decapitated body in sight, she found it was easier for her to think about what they were there for, rather than constantly being distracted by the macabre sights.

'Well, let's examine the evidence we have so far. The decapitated body of Douglas Norton, a local butcher, is found in an alleyway near his home. His head is then found at his workplace,' Sam began to reel off enthusiastically, 'his abdomen was marked with a sigil, and the Void sigil was found beneath his severed head. Now, there was no sign of a struggle where the body was found, and there's no evidence of a forced entry to the butcher's shop. What would that suggest to you?' He span around again, pointing at Alice to answer his question as if this was some kind of murder mystery pop-quiz.

'That Douglas trusted whoever killed him? He wouldn't have struggled against his attacker, because he wouldn't have seen it coming. He must've also trusted whoever it was with a set of keys to the shop, so maybe a co-worker?' She was uncertain she was right, but it was the first thought that popped into her head.

'A sound theory, but the attacker could easily have taken the keys off of the body. Nevertheless, Mister Norton was stabbed in the front – not from behind – and *then* decapitated, but didn't seem to put up much of a struggle. And they knew enough about him to know he worked here, and what time he would be heading back home. It's likely that whoever it was was someone he recognised and probably trusted, like a friend or associate.' Sam said, and he continued to case the interior of the shop. He still couldn't see anything else of interest, but felt like he was missing something important.

'And what about the symbols? Why have all three bodies been found with the same sigil?' Alice asked.

'Same murderer, same motive,' he replied, gazing absently out of the window.

'Which is?'

'Haven't the foggiest.'

'Brilliant.' Alice had hoped for something a bit more insightful, especially from a self-proclaimed detective.

'All I do know is that they were cast for some dark intent,' Sam said.

'Three murders with mutilated corpses; a dark intent behind it? You surprise me!' She pulled a sarcastic "I'm-incredibly-surprised" face.

'There must be a reason the murderer chose these three victims... This is more than a murder of convenience, especially now that Mister Norton's head was found here,' Sam said, although he seemed to be pondering things out-loud more than talking to anyone directly. 'No... Your run-of-the-mill killer wouldn't go to the effort of decapitating his victim and leaving the head in the window display, it's too... Unnecessary. Not to mention the sigil carvings in all of the victims, too. That's more than just a signature or a boast.'

'So what are you thinking? That someone wanted these men out of the picture for whatever reason?'

'Yes, and not just any reason. One doesn't cast a sigil without an intent, and this symbol wasn't carved into the Void crystal for no reason. There's definitely something supernatural behind all of this, and I think I know what it is.'

'Which is?' Alice was getting tired of Sam's vague musings.

'Well, we haven't got all the evidence yet, but it's a good starting point. Mister Norton here, and the other recently deceased, may very well have been part of a cult and perhaps – perhaps – they may have been the unwitting sacrificial goats in a blood magick ritual they didn't even know they were participating in. Using blood magick to cast Void sigils would, to me, suggest trying to bring some physicality to something metaphysical, which isn't a particularly good plan.' He spun on his feet and made a b-line for the door.

'So what now? We go in search of a murderous cultist maniac practising some kind of dangerous dark magick?'

'No,' Sam said, turning to face Alice, 'we're going to talk to people, ask around, see if anyone knows whether or not Mister Norton or his fellow victims were involved in some sinister and arcane organisation. *Then* we're going to go in search of a murderous cultist maniac practising dangerous dark magick.'

Outside the butcher's shop, Officer Smith was talking with the man behind the wheel of the black van. The man seemed to be wearing a well tailored black suit, and a pair of dark sunglasses covered his eyes. Sam thought this was odd for two reasons. Firstly, that such a good suit wasn't really suitable for handling severed heads. Secondly, it wasn't remotely sunny enough to be wearing sunglasses. He gave Officer Smith a cursory wave as he and Alice walked by, but Smith and the other man were too busy to notice. Instead, Sam approached two of the other attending officers.

'Excuse me. Hi. I was just wondering, have you managed to identify any potential suspects, maybe familial or social connections to the victim yet?'

The officers stared back at him with stone-like expressions. 'Isn't that your job, detective?' One of them asked him flatly.

'Well, yes, but I've been investigating the victim's workplace, not sifting through files,' Sam said indignantly, reasserting himself as the one in charge here. He straightened himself, sizing up to the two officers, and clutched at his coat's lapels.

'An ID was found on the body at the initial crime scene. A background check should have been run by now.'

One of the officers nodded, and reached down for his radio. 'McKenzie to dispatch, have you got backgrounds on the Grimditch body?' The radio squawked an incoherent response through the static. 'Copy that,' he said after several garbled sentences. Sam still couldn't get his head around how any of these policemen were able to understand what was being said. 'Ex-wife, Felicity Bamford. Lives a few roads away from the victim's house. We've yet to notify her of her ex-husband's passing.'

'Thank you, Officer McKenzie,' Sam nodded, 'if it's all the same to you, I'll be the one to break the news to her. I have a few questions I'd like to ask her.'

'Yes, sir. She lives at 74 Prior Road,' Officer McKenzie said. 'Mind your backs,' he added as the black van slowly approached them, and Sam and Alice stepped out of the way for it to pass.

'Thank you,' Sam said after the van had passed, 'be sure to inform me as soon as we have a search warrant for Mister Norton's property.' He was actually starting to quite enjoy the proper-police-detective act, severed heads notwithstanding. 'Come on,' he said to Alice as he started to walk down the road, 'we've got bad news to break.'

Chapter III

Sam and Alice made their way up the garden path to the front door of Felicity Bamford's home. It was a fairly old looking house, probably having stood on this road for at least seventy years. The wooden window frames were decaying, their white paint peeling away to reveal the damp wood beneath, and the blue door was starting to show signs of weathering. Sam knocked rhythmically on the door, and stuck his hands in his pockets as they waited. A few moments passed, and the door slowly creaked open. A woman's face peered tentatively around the corner. 'Hello?' She greeted them warily.

'Felicity Bamford?' Sam asked, inching his foot towards the threshold.

'Yes...?' Felicity Bamford replied with a nod.

'I'm Sam Hain, and this is my friend and associate, Alice Carroll -'

'Hello,' Alice chimed in.

'Hi,' Felicity said with a half-smile.

'- we're working with the Metropolitan Police,' Sam continued, pulling out his fake police ID, 'your ex-husband was Douglas Norton?'

Felicity nodded uncertainly. 'Yes,' she said, confused and concerned about where this was going.

'We have some bad news. May we come in?'

'Oh Christ...' Felicity took a step back, her face now wrought with concern. 'What's Doug done?'

'Not much, he's dead.' Sam said matter-of-factly. Alice suddenly regretted not suggesting to him that she be the one to break the delicate news. The words "delicate" and "Sam Hain" rarely fell within the same sentence. Except for that one.

'Wha-? How?' The colour drained from Felicity's face, turning ashen and wan.

'Miss Bamford,' Alice said, taking a step forward and pushing past Sam, 'if we could please come in we'd just like to talk to you for a bit. We're terribly sorry for your loss.' She shot a quick, scolding look at Sam.

'Yes, very sorry.' Sam nodded in agreement, but he sounded more like a toddler who'd just been told off than a man offering his condolences.

'Oh, of course. Sorry. Please, come in,' Felicity said obligingly, opening the door wide for them. Her face was now almost as white as her house, and she had a distant, worried look in her eyes.

Felicity led Sam and Alice into her living room and directed them to be seated. It was a fairly sparse room, of cream carpet and walls, the furniture pointing towards the television, and a modest array of ornaments sat atop the mantelpiece above the gas fireplace. Felicity hovered around Sam and Alice for a brief moment, not sure what to do with herself.

'Can I get you two a cup of tea?' She eventually asked, her voice trembling.

'No, it's quite all right,' Alice said, and gestured for her to sit also, 'are you okay? Maybe I can get *you* a cup of tea?'

'I'm fine. Really,' Felicity said, lowering herself into an armchair, 'I'm just... shocked. You know?' Alice nodded sympathetically.

'So when was the last time you saw Douglas?' Sam asked, leaning forward and attempting to soften his voice.

'Only last week. We tried to stay friends after things didn't work out, but... Things are never quite as they used to be, I suppose. How did it... How did it happen?' Felicity asked.

'We're not quite sure of all the details, but we're dealing with a murder,' Sam said.

'*Murder*,' Felicity whispered involuntarily with shock.

'Indeed. I'll spare you the details,' he said, 'we just need to ask you a few questions, if you can answer them as best you can.'

Alice reached out and held Felicity by the hand. She could feel her shaking. 'I know this is difficult, but please try and stay calm and remember everything you can about last night.'

Felicity nodded, 'okay.'

'Well, first of all, where were you last night?' Sam asked, pulling out a pen and notepad. He stared intently at Felicity.

'I was here, at home,' she replied.

'Was anyone here with you last night?' Alice asked. 'The police want to cover all angles, and we'd like to save you any unnecessary stress.'

'Um, no. No. I was here alone.'

'Listen, Miss Bamford, I'm not here to interrogate you, or catch you out or whatever. I'm following my own... let's say *unique* line of investigation, and I'm just looking for information which could point me in the right direction. I trust you – I do – but the police will need something to support your alibi, otherwise they'll label you a suspect.' Sam said. 'I believe that your ex-husband's murder is connected with the two other deaths which have occurred this month, and the police can't ignore the similarities between the cases. If you have anything which might prove you either weren't responsible for Douglas Norton's murder-' Felicity let out a slight whimper at the words '- or have a solid alibi for the nights of any of the other victims, it'll help you immensely.'

'I remember when I heard the news about the first one,' she began to explain, 'because I thought to myself, *Christ, that's where I live!*'

'Where were you when you heard the news of the first murder? What were you doing around the time of Elliot Ferguson's death?'

'I was on a team-building weekend, up in Peterborough-'

'Oh, how frightfully dull,' Sam interrupted. 'I'm sorry, carry on.'

'When you find out that someone was

murdered just down the road from where you live, it makes you grateful you're not at home. You don't feel quite as safe in your own town when that happens.'

'And the second murder. Brian Mayweather, I believe. Where were you when that happened?'

'That was around the 10th, wasn't it?' Felicity asked, and Sam nodded in confirmation. 'That was the night of Doug's party. His birthday was on the 8th, and he invited a group of friends to join him at *The Hog's Head* on the Friday night for drinks.'

'And the others who were there can confirm this?' Alice asked.

'Yes. I can give you their details if you want?' Felicity said. She was starting to settle down a bit more, probably because the questioning was keeping her occupied and distracted from the shock of Douglas's passing.

'That would be most helpful, thank you Miss Bamford,' Sam said. 'I know that you and Douglas have been separated for a while, but were you aware of Douglas's whereabouts last night?'

Felicity hesitated momentarily, gathering her thoughts. 'Not as such, no,' she replied uneasily, 'but he used to go to the pub every Wednesday and Friday night and meet up with some friends. At a guess, I'd say he was there.'

'Would you happen to know who he was with last night?' Sam probed.

'I don't know everyone my ex-husband was friends with, detective. He was friendly with almost everyone in Grimditch.'

'You say "almost",' Sam pried a little more, 'was there anyone Douglas was not friendly with?'

'Oh no, I don't mean it in that way,' Felicity answered, somewhat flustered, 'I only meant that I don't *know* everyone in Grimditch.'

'Okay, I understand. But if you can think of anyone who might have wanted your ex-husband dead...'

Felicity shook her head morosely. She and Douglas had had their ups and downs, but even in the heat of an argument she wouldn't have wished this upon him, and she certainly couldn't think of anyone who would have wanted to kill him.

'No,' she uttered, 'a lot of people liked Doug. He was the local butcher, always friendly and happy to see his regular customers. He was very sociable. I can't think of anyone who would want to...' Her sentence trailed off.

Sam had been taking notes of everything Felicity had been saying, nodding and hmm-ing attentively. He scrawled the last few notes into his moleskine notebook before looking back up at her. 'Now this might strike you as an odd question, but was your ex-husband involved in any kind of group or organisation? Maybe like a society, or gang, or something?'

'A gang? No, no, he was never part of a gang or anything. As I said, he met up with a group of friends at the pub a couple of times a week, but that was it.'

'Do you know if he was involved with the occult in anyway? Applied the arcane arts?

Meddled with magick not meant for mortal men?' Sam enquired, particularly fond of his last sentence. *I might use that one more often...*

'What? What kind of-? N-no, of course not. Why?'

'We suspect it may have played a part in his murder, and those of the other victims this past month.' He reclined into the soft, cushiony back of the sofa, appearing to write down some more well-considered thoughts in his notepad. In fact, he was now just doodling; it helped him think. He scribbled a rough copy of the sigils found on Douglas's body, and eyed it with a wary eye.

'Well, he did have an interest in conspiracy theories and secret societies, but it was only an interest of his. I don't think he was ever *involved* in any, not anything that would put his life at risk. He and Pete used to debate about crazy conspiracies all the time.'

'Who's Pete?' Alice asked. Sam stopped scribbling and looked up, intrigued.

'Pete Jones. He and Doug worked together for a while. Pete left the butcher's to work at a delicatessen down the road, but he still popped in to help Doug out and cover the shop if he needed to,' Felicity paused for a moment, but Sam's eagerly enquiring face pressed her for more information. 'They'd talk at length about all kinds of weird stuff.'

'Such as...?'

'Oh I don't know, I never really listened to any of it. The usual conspiracy stuff I suppose; secret organisations running the world, controlling the state of the economy; aliens working with the American government, and spaceships disguised as clouds.' Felicity giggled to herself, remembering some of the mad things Douglas used to say. Her fond memories started to bring a little bit of colour back into her otherwise pale face.

'Any idea where I might be able to find this Pete Jones? We're going to need to speak to him also.'

'He'll probably be at work at the delicatessen. You don't think he's responsible, do you? He's a bit of a joker and can be quite pig-headed, but he's okay.'

'No. Well, not yet. Too soon to say either way, really. We just need to build up a profile of your ex-husband's life, it might help us draw some connections and come close to identifying his killer. Anyway,' Sam said, pocketing his notepad, 'thank you for your cooperation, Miss Bamford. Again, we're terribly sorry for your loss.'

As Sam stood up, he noticed something on the mantelpiece. It was a small, circular stone, probably no larger than a fifty-pence piece. Carved into the front of it was a symbol, an angular hieroglyph with a right-slanting line at the top, and a long vertical line stretching downwards, ending in a two-pronged fork shape. The carved symbol had been carefully painted in gold, making it stand out from the slate-like stone, and Sam thought he vaguely recognised it from some ancient culture. *Possibly Egypt*, he thought. He couldn't explain why it had caught his eye, but he felt compelled to take a closer look.

'Oh, cool stone,' he remarked, and walked over to the mantelpiece to have a better look at it. It was curiously, almost unnaturally, smooth, and the more he looked at it the more he was sure it was an Ancient Egyptian symbol. He felt like he'd seen it before at any rate.

In fact, now that he was sure it was Egyptian, he could see other pieces of Egyptian symbolism and memorabilia around the room, such as the statue of a serpent-like creature, and another which was a weird amalgamation of creatures, with the head of a crocodile, the forequarters of a lion and the hindquarters of a hippopotamus. *Ancient Egypt had some cool looking gods.* 'Been to Egypt recently by any chance?' He asked, turning back to face Felicity.

'No, I haven't. My boyfriend went last month though,' she replied dismissively, 'Ryan came back with a suitcase full of weird little trinkets like that.'

'If you don't mind me asking, did Ryan and Douglas get on? You said you tried to stay friendly with Douglas after the divorce, so that must have caused some tension with you and your boyfriend?'

'Not really, the two of them actually got on quite well. They had a lot of things in common. They'd even go for a pint together sometimes.'

'Hmm, then he's a better man than me! I wouldn't want to go for a drink with my ex's new boyfriend,' Sam said. 'So, just to be sure, Ryan wouldn't have any motive to kill Douglas?'

'No! Of course not.'

'Okay, just checking,' Sam said, a sceptical tone in his voice, and he turned to leave. 'Thank you again for your cooperation, Miss Bamford. We'll be in touch when we have more information or if we need to ask you any more questions.'

'Oh, all right,' Felicity replied, and she stood up to escort Sam and Alice to the front door. She opened the door for the two of them, and with a wave goodbye she said 'thank you for letting me know, detective. I appreciate what you're doing. Just get this guy.'

'It's very much my intention to,' Sam replied without even turning around to face her, and with a casual wave over his shoulder he carried on striding down the path. Alice put her arm reassuringly around Felicity's shoulders as she went to leave, and handed her a piece of paper with several numbers written on it.

'I quickly looked up the details for some local bereavement counsellors,' she said as Felicity took the paper, 'I'm sure the police will have somebody for you to talk to, too, but I thought... You know.'

Felicity nodded and smiled slightly. 'Thank you,' she said, and Alice thought she could see Felicity's eyes welling up with tears. With a quick hug and a final goodbye, Alice stepped down the stone steps and walked down the garden path to join Sam.

'So what's the plan, Batman?' Alice asked once Felicity had shut the door. 'We've got a couple of names now, where shall we start?'

Sam gazed off into the middle-distance as he thought for a moment. 'Hmm, yes. Pete Jones and Felicity's new boyfriend Ryan... We'll start with Mister Jones. If Douglas Norton was dabbling in conspiracies and the occult, Pete Jones would probably know.' He started to walk down the road, only to suddenly stop after a few steps, and he turned to face Alice. 'And don't call me Batman. If I were a comic book character, I've always fancied myself more of a *Constantine* type.'

'But that doesn't even rhyme!' Alice said.

'Doug's... dead?' Pete Jones said in utter disbelief, resting his head in his palm as he leaned on the counter of the east London delicatessen. He was a middle-aged man, succumbing to the effects of a gradually greying and receding hairline, and his face was creased with grief. His apron and gloves were marred with flecks of grease, and Sam and Alice had immediately been able to identify him by a small badge pinned to his chest which read "Hello! My name is Pete" secured to his apron with a small, gold pin. 'How?' He asked after a few moments silence.

'We're attempting to find that out, Mister Jones. We spoke with Felicity a few hours ago, and she suggested that you might know more about Douglas's recent circumstances. When was the last time you and he saw each other?' Sam asked. He leaned against the delicatessen's counter, and immediately regretted it when he felt an unidentifiable cold liquid seeping into the elbow of his coat.

'Well, we used to work together, but ever since I took the job here we've met up like twice, three times a week,' Pete said.

'Yes, Felicity mentioned that. But when did you last see Douglas?' Alice asked. She didn't repeat Sam's mistake of leaning and putting her elbow in some anonymous fluid, and instead decided to stay standing upright.

'Last night. Ryan and I met up with him at *The Hog's Head* for a couple of pints,' he replied. 'Guess that was shortly before...'

'I'm afraid so, yes,' Sam said with a solemn nod. 'Was there anything that stood out to you last night? Someone at the pub who you might not have seen there before, maybe someone who left at the same time as Douglas?'

'No, not that I saw. Most of the regulars were in, nothin' out of the ordinary.' Pete replied.

'And what about Doug? Did he seem off-colour, a little distracted or worried about something?' Alice asked.

'He looked tired, but other than that, no.'

'Hmm, okay. And you mentioned that a Ryan was there with you last night. Would this perchance be the same Ryan as is currently in a relationship with Miss Felicity Bamford?' Sam enquired with an inquisitive raise of the eyebrow.

'Yeah, Ryan Nicholls. That's how Flick met him; me, Doug 'n' him go way back.'

'As I understand it, you liked to discuss things of a slightly unconventional nature?'

'What, Flick told you 'bout the things they like in the bedroom?' Pete seemed genuinely shocked, and more than a little embarrassed.

'Um, no... No. She mentioned the conspiracy theory stuff, though.' Sam shifted uncomfortably.

'Oh, right. Pretend I didn't mention bedroom stuff. Shouldn't be tellin' officers of the law about a man's private bits.'

'I wouldn't mind ignoring the subject, either,' Alice added.

'Anyway, conspiracy theories, the occult...' Sam prompted.

'Wasn't anythin' really. Just discussed ideas and theories about stuff, shared things we'd read online. Was just interesting to think about, really.'

'And have you or Douglas ever practised the occult or dabbled in magick?'

Pete was silent for a few seconds, a look of confusion across his face. 'No, no. Why, y'think that could have something to do with Doug's death? That's madder than some of the tinfoil hat crackpot theories we'd read about!'

'I have my theories, Mister Jones. So neither of you belonged to any secret societies or cults or anything?'

'What, and if we was you think I'd tell ya?!' Pete said with a half-hearted smile. Sam simply stared at him. 'Nah, course not,' Pete added, 'was only jokin'.'

'What about Ryan Nicholls? What can you tell me about him?' Sam asked, taking down a few hastily scrawled notes into his notebook.

'He's a banker, works in the Shard. Doug sometimes felt like Flick had traded him in for a wealthier man, but he seemed alright with it.'

'And there was no bad blood between them? No hard feelings about having been with the same woman?'

'Nah. For a man and his ex's new fella, the two of them got on like a house on fire. There'd be the occasional comment, but they was just joshin'. And Flick and Doug still got on alright after the divorce.'

'So you wouldn't say that Ryan would want to have Douglas killed?' Alice asked.

'No, he wouldn't. He's not that kind of guy. Yeah, sure, in a soap opera or somethin' then they'd've been arch-enemies, but it wasn't like that at all.'

'An-' Sam started to say, but was quickly interrupted.

'And no, before you ask, Ryan is not in a cult or some master voodoo sorcerer.'

'I wasn't actually going to ask that, but thank you for the additional information, Mister Jones,' Sam said. 'I was actually going to ask where I might be able to find Ryan now. You and he were with Douglas last night, and I'd like to ask him a few questions too.'

'Oh, well he's out of town on business today, but he'll probably be at home tomorrow,' Pete replied, scratching at the back of his head awkwardly. 'How's Flick handlin' things, anyways? She holdin' up alright?'

'She'll be okay, she was very taken aback by the shock when we broke the news to her, and she'll need to take time to mourn,' Alice said, and Pete nodded with a solemn agreement, 'I left her with the numbers for several bereavement counsellors, and I'm sure the police will have some contacts too.'

'Could I, uh... Could I also have the numbers of them counsellors?' Pete asked hesitantly, and his already ruddy complexion turned slightly redder. Alice nodded, and handed him a piece of paper – evidently she'd made a couple of copies just in case. Pete muttered a 'thanks' and quickly pocketed the paper.

'Thank you for your time, Mister Jones,' Sam said with a courteous tip of the hat, and he proceeded to walk towards the door.

'No worries, guv'. I hope you get the guy,' Pete said, regaining his composure.

As they were about to walk out of the delicatessen, Alice turned around. 'Sorry, one more question Pete?'

'Yeah?' He looked up from the counter.

'Did you happen to know any of the other murder victims from around this area? Have you lost any other friends or colleagues this month?'

'Yeah, I knew Brian. Mayweather. He used to join us down the pub for a couple of pints on a Friday. Things've been quieter since...'

'I'm sorry, it can't be easy for you. Both Douglas and Brian were found in very similar circumstances, as was the other victim,' Alice stated.

'I... I didn't know that. You think they were got by the same guy?'

'It's a theory we haven't ruled out,' Sam replied, 'now, we've got work to do.' He strode purposefully out of the door, and beckoned for Alice to follow.

'Two good friends gone in the same month...' Pete said morosely to himself as Sam and Alice left the delicatessen. 'Christ.'

Standing outside of the delicatessen, Sam quickly checked the time on his phone. It was now early afternoon, and he still hadn't heard anything about a search warrant for Douglas Norton's house. Aside from questioning Ryan Nicholls, it was the only thing Sam could think of that might lead him towards an answer. Something about the case made him feel uneasy, and it wasn't just the murder. There was something else, something important he was missing, but he couldn't quite put his finger on it. A gust of wind came blowing down Grimditch high street and threatened to steal Sam's hat. He clung on to the wide brims and tipped it further down in front of his face. No force of nature was going to take his beloved hat.

'Why didn't you want to ask him about Brian Mayweather?' Alice asked as she stepped out of the shop and joined Sam. 'Surely that would've helped us in some way?'

'Probably not. We already know Pete Jones is not a man for great detail, and he'd already confirmed that Mister Mayweather joined them at the pub prior to his murder. But where does that leave Elliot Ferguson in this picture? The fact that only some, not all, of the victims were friends means we can't rely on there being a social connection. If we can solve why one was murdered, we may well have the reason for the remaining two as well, and that will in turn lead us to a conclusion,' Sam surmised.

'If you say so, I just thought it might be worth following up. So, what's the scheme, Constantine?'

'I like that one!' Sam said with an approving smile. 'Well, we can try to get in touch with Ryan Nicholls, which might be difficult with him out of town. Seems a little convenient he was around yesterday, but not today...' He paused to think for a moment, staring up into the light grey sky as he tried to come up with an idea. 'It'd be an idea to rummage through the previous case files for both Ferguson and Mayweather, they might provide us with a connection. We'll need to head to the police station anyway to start trying to get in touch with Mister Nicholls.'

'Okay, where's the station?'

'I have no idea...' As Sam went to reach for his phone to check a map, he felt his pocket vibrate. Pulling out his phone and unlocking it in one quick motion, he opened his new message. *Have the warrant for Douglas Norton's house,* the message read, *meet outside 26 Becknall Crescent. -Smith*

'Looks like we're going to Douglas's for afternoon tea,' Sam said.

Douglas Norton's place wasn't much to look at. It was a small house, a simple two-up-two-down building with a basic garden towards the back of it. The police had already arrived by the time Sam and Alice got there, and they were busy investigating the inside of the house. Not wanting to miss out on any of the snooping around, Sam immediately bounded up the door step into 26 Becknall Crescent.

Inside, Douglas's house was in a state of disarray. House-keeping was evidently not one of his strong points. The carpets were thick and darkened in spots with dust and trodden-in dirt, and the coffee table in the middle of the living room was covered with scrunched up receipts, loose change and torn-open letters; a half-full and long abandoned coffee mug sat resting on top of this pile of scrap paper. None of the furniture matched, clearly bought more for function than appearance, and there was no discernible sense of order or tidiness to the place.

Sam started to case the room, looking around and scanning for anything vaguely useful in his investigation. It was clear Douglas Norton didn't consider his home-life a priority, but Sam hoped there might be some evidence around here which he could connect with the supernatural or the occult. He started to rummage through the piles of paper on the coffee table, turning over outstanding bills and bank statements with little interest, and picked up a copy of the *Evening Standard*. It was a couple of days old, marked with the occasional coffee stain, and open with the crossword facing upwards. Some of the words had been filled in, each letter appeared slightly shaky, as if written on a train or in a car, but evidently Douglas Norton hadn't had the time to finish it. Sam stared at the paper, and was momentarily distracted when he absent-mindedly started to wonder about the frankly obscure and cryptic clue for 20 Down, *Earl in indiscriminate use of rubber.*

'Hey, have a look at this,' Alice said from the other end of the room, leaning over a table with another inexplicably large pile of paper, 'looks like Douglas left his laptop on.'

Douglas's laptop had indeed been left turned on, charging and sitting on stand-by. As Alice opened the laptop up, the screen came to life; it was already signed into Douglas's user account, the front window of his butcher's shop set as the desktop background. In the image, sitting prominently in the middle window and surrounded by hanging porcine carcasses, was a pig's head. Its mouth was clasped around a shiny red apple, and its eyes were partially concealed by a pair of novelty sunglasses. A Hawaiian-style sun-hat rested upon its head, and a wreath of fake pink flowers were wrapped around its neck. Sam peered over Alice's shoulder at the screen.

'Huh, how's that for irony...'

'I know! What is it you say about

coincidences?' She said, turning to him.

'That there's no such thing, the Universe is rarely so lazy?'

'That's the one. Yeah, it can't be coincidence that this is exactly what happened to Douglas...'

'Not at all. Almost a fitting send-off for Mister Norton, don't you think?'

Alice didn't respond, she just carried on looking at the screen, sifting through the recently used programs. At the very top of the menu sat a short-cut to Douglas Norton's emails and, out of investigative curiosity, she clicked it.

Douglas Norton's email account was as much of a mess as his house; his inbox was flooded with spam emails, unopened newsletters and social media notifications. But in amongst it all was something which stood out considerably, and immediately caught both Alice's and Sam's attention. It was an email conversation, no subject line, between three correspondents; Douglas Norton, Elliot Ferguson, and Brian Mayweather.

Sam pointed to the screen. 'Click th-'

'Yeah, yeah, I saw that, just opening it...'

The conversation opened in a new window, showing the email thread between the three men. The first message was received on the 2nd of January. Some of the emails in the thread were now missing, presumably deleted from the conversation for reasons best known only to the person who deleted them, but what remained of the email exchange read as follows.

From: elliotferg@mail.com
To: brian.mayweather@mail.com, norton72@mail.com
Subject: Re: no subject
*I've been thinking about the artefact.....I don't know what
it is about it, but it fascinates me in a disturbing way.
There's something haunting and unsettling, almost other-
worldly about it, I can't explain it. It's only been sat on the
shelf a couple of days, but it makes me feel uneasy whenever
I look at it. Feels like it's watching me, you know?*

From: brian.mayweather@mail.com
To: elliotferg@mail.com, norton72@mail.com
Subject: Re: no subject
*You're just imagining things, it's fine. We're not even sure
what it represents yet. When I'm next at the Lodge, I'll dig
through the archives and see if I can find any references to
it. In the meantime, we just need to keep it somewhere safe.*

'Check out Brian's user image,' Alice said, as
she stared at the screen. Brian Mayweather's
profile picture was a black square with a simple
gold pattern in the middle. It was an angular
shape, with a right-slanting line at the top and a
long vertical line stretching downwards, ending in
a two-pronged fork shape. 'I've seen that
somewhere before.'

Sam nodded in agreement. 'Felicity Bamford's
mantelpiece...'

'I think there was something like that in
Douglas's wallet, too,' Alice added, thinking back
to the beginning of the day. The token in Douglas
Norton's wallet did bare a striking resemblance to
the piece on Felicity's mantelpiece, and in Brian's
user image. 'Another not-at-all-coincidence?'

'Certainly not,' Sam replied. He reached over Alice's shoulder, tapping impatiently at the arrow keys to continue reading the rest of the emails.

From: elliotferg@mail.com
To: brian.mayweather@mail.com, norton72@mail.com
Subject: Re: no subject
OK, but can we please not keep it in my house? I cant even stand being in the same room as it any more. Dont want to sound mad, but I think its evil. It whispers to me at night in my dreams. Can we please move it somewhere else?

There was a gap in the thread, as if several of the intermediate emails had been deleted from the conversation. The messages picked up again on the 5th of January.

From: norton72@mail.com
To: elliotferg@mail.com, brian.mayweather@mail.com
Subject: Re: no subject
The Regents like to use scare-tactics so we don't take any of their precious artefacts. It's mostly harmless. We're getting close, though.

From: brian.mayweather@mail.com
To: elliotferg@mail.com, norton72@mail.com
Subject: Re: no subject
I'll take it back to mine after the next session, see if I can get anything else from it.

The thread ended there, with no further contact evident between the three parties; although, with the amount of missing messages in-between, any further emails may also have been deleted. However, there was one additional email outside of the conversation, dated the 9th of

January. Alice clicked on it and began to read.

From: brian.mayweather@mail.com
To: norton72@mail.com
Subject: no subject
*Douglas, it got Elliot, and now it's coming for me. I can
hear something banging on the door, and trying to break in.
Every night I can hear it clawing at my windows. I can't
see it, but I know it's there. It's hiding in the shadows,
watching, waiting. It's that damn artefact... We should
never have given that blood offering. I think it wants more.
We've got to get rid of it. I've sent the artefact to your shop,
hopefully it going through the post will put it off the scent.*

'Rub a dub dub, three fools in a tub. And who
do you think they be?' Sam chanted in a sing-song
kind of voice.

'The butcher, the baker, the candlestick
maker...' Alice mused as she continued to glance
over Douglas Norton's inbox.

'Turn them out, knaves all three!' He declared
with a flourish. 'Looks like they were all meddling
with something they really shouldn't have been
meddling with. Blood offerings, never a wise
move. Give a drop of your blood to an entity, and
it will just keep on wanting more. Offer your life-
force to a demon powerful enough, and it won't
hesitate to come after you and claim its tribute.
Especially if they were toying with something they
didn't know anything about.'

'What are you thinking?' Alice asked, turning
away from the screen for a moment to look at
Sam.

'Some kind of supernatural souvenir by the

sounds of it, most likely an Akashic artefact,' he replied, stroking his chin in thought.

'Akashic artefact?'

'An artefact imbued with Akasha energy,' Sam said helpfully. 'It might bestow some kind of metaphysical or supernatural power, or change the energy of an area around it with its mere presence. If they were giving blood offerings to a demonic force through this thing... Who knows what they could have unleashed. And who are these "Regents"?'

'Hang on, there's something to Pete in the sent folder,' Alice said, and she opened the email. It was dated yesterday, the 22nd of January.

From: norton72@mail.com
To: p.jones@mail.com
Subject: favour
Pete, I need you to come to the shop soon, maybe this Friday after a pint, to pick up something. It's something more than either of us could've imagined! I'll explain more at the pub later, but you won't regret it. Thanks, bud, I'll owe you one.

'See? Told you we should've questioned Pete a bit more,' Alice said triumphantly, an "I-told-you-so" look crossing her face. Sam nodded in agreement.

'All right, you're right. Looks like we'll have to pay Mister Jones another visit then; he knows more than he's letting on.'

'That might be a little difficult,' came the voice of Officer Smith from somewhere behind them, and Sam quickly closed Douglas's laptop. 'We tried to call him in for an official statement, but we can't find him anywhere. He's not at work or at his home. We're running a trace on his Oyster card now to see if he's travelling anywhere, and we've got feelers out looking for him.'

'Any word on Felicity Bamford or Ryan Nicholls?' Sam asked.

'Miss Bamford has been very obliging, and her alibis check out. We've yet to reach Nicholls at work or on his mobile, seems he always disappears around these times.'

'Wait, what do you mean "always around these times"?' Alice asked curiously.

'Nicholls has always been a contact for each of the deceased, so we've had to bring him in for questioning on a number of occasions. But every time he's been away on business the day after the incident,' Officer Smith explained. 'Seems suspicious to me, but his alibis have been consistently solid, and there's no evidence whatsoever which can pin him to any of the murders. I guess he's just a very unlucky guy.'

'Hmm, seems off to me too, but unless we have something solid to go on there's nothing we can do,' Sam mused. 'If it's all right with you, officer, I'd like to review some of the previous case files and see if I can find anything which can give us a lead.'

'Sure thing, detective. I'll have a ride dispatched shortly,' replied Officer Smith, and he walked away mumbling into his radio.

Outside of the house, Sam waited for the police car to turn up and take him to the station. He was trying to think of the best course of action to take, with both Ryan and Pete nowhere to be found, they were now feeling their way around in the dark. He was just clinging on to whatever he could find which might lead him towards a conclusion. He couldn't shake the feeling that he was close to something, building up a picture of the circumstances surrounding the deaths, but no solid answers.

If what these men had been doing had caught the attention of something, and that something had been summoned through blood offerings, Sam wondered, gazing pensively up at the grey skies, *would that something not seek to claim every drop of blood it could get? Would it be satisfied with taking just the lives of the ones who summoned it, or would it crave more?*

'Alice,' Sam eventually said, returning his focus back down to Earth, 'while I'm digging through the files, stay here with the police. Start going through all of Douglas's emails, see if you can find any further reference to the artefact, or to the Regents.' He returned his gaze to the sky. 'Plus, I'd be happier knowing you're safe here for the moment.'

'Okay, and then what?' Alice didn't feel like he was trying to cut her out of the case this time; she was actually quite pleased he was trusting her with conducting one side of the investigation while he was busy with another.

'I'll give you a text when I'm done, and we'll reconvene later,' he said, and waved to the police car as it turned the corner into Becknall Crescent. 'I'll see you later. Keep in contact if you find anything.'

'I will,' Alice replied, 'see you in a bit.'

The message had come through about four hours after Sam left for the station. It was brief and to the point.

Meet at butcher's after dark. Will explain more later. -SH

CHAPTER IV

Alice pulled her jacket tightly around herself as she walked down Grimditch high street. The cold night air was especially bitter this evening, and the skies were pitch black – not a single star was in sight. Small groups of people wandered about the road, marching from pub to pub on a Thursday night crawl (quite why pubs were now more popular on Thursdays than on Fridays, Alice didn't know), but every now and again the evening would fall eerily still, not a single soul in sight. Alice didn't really know which one she'd rather, the creepy empty streets or the equally creepy stares she was getting from groups of men on a night out. She was relieved when she saw the familiar figure of a man in an overcoat and a fedora hat leaning against a lamp post. Sam looked more noir-like than ever, his figure silhouetted against the dim orange glow of the street light.

'Evening,' Sam said as Alice approached, and he took a few steps forward from the lamp post. 'How'd you get on?'

'Not too bad, actually,' Alice replied., and she waved a memory stick in front of him. 'I've downloaded Douglas's emails, but they don't really add much more to what we read earlier.'

'Nothing more about the Regents?'

'Not really, the Regents are only mentioned a few times in passing. But, I did find out more about that symbol.'

'Oh?'

'I did a quick search for it. It's the Was Sceptre, an Ancient Egyptian symbol held by Gods and Kings. Apparently it represents power, dominion, and – you've probably guessed this – regency.'

'Interesting...'

'What'd you find out?'

'Well, it turns out that both Mayweather and Ferguson had similar tokens to the ones found in Norton's wallet, and Nicholls's piece on Bamford's mantelpiece. If the Was Sceptre is the logo of the Regents, then I think we have a solid connection between the three victims and Ryan Nicholls,' Sam said. 'Also, Ryan was consistently away on business the day after each murder. As Smith said, his alibis check out. Every time he returned to town, he was brought in for questioning, but there's never been enough evidence to tie him to any of the cases, aside from him being generally suspicious and cagey. However, the day after each of the times he's been questioned, the houses of the victims have been broken into and ransacked, but nothing was taken or missing from the victims' personal effects. The detective reports from each of these incidents indicate that the perpetrator was looking for something, but couldn't find it.'

'So why was Douglas's house – well, it wasn't "okay", it was a mess – but why hadn't it been broken into too?'

'Ryan Nicholls is out of town, the break-ins only occurred after he returned. I'd like to talk to him about those when the police bring him in tomorrow.'

'Why are we meeting back here then?' Alice asked, looking up at the butcher's shop. It looked strange and eerie in the dim evening light, illuminated only by the light from the lamp post, and as she peered through the window she could see long, haunting shadows stretching towards the back of the shop, disappearing into the darkness.

'Douglas's email to Pete indicated he had something here. I felt like something was off when we were first here, and it wasn't just the severed head. We're missing something important, and I think that artefact is here, somewhere,' Sam said. He walked towards the door of the butcher's shop, quickly looked over each shoulder, and leaned forward to pick the lock. Alice peered around nervously. She heard scraping, turning, prying, and then a satisfying click. Sam stood up and grinned at her.

'Shall we go in then?'

The little bell jingled cheerily as Sam slowly pushed the door open, stepping into the butcher's shop. The place was partially lit by the street lights outside, but towards the back of the shop was nothing but a thick veil of blackness. That distinct smell of a butcher's shop, of dead flesh and slowly decaying meat, hung heavily in the air, and Alice felt her stomach turn as the pungent aroma hit her nostrils.

'Remind me why we're breaking into a smelly butcher's shop in the middle of the night?' she whispered to Sam.

'Because,' he replied, not bothering to whisper, 'I can conduct *my* investigation properly without the police peering over my shoulders.'

'I know, but... Couldn't we have at least stuck roses up our noses?'

'Bit prickly.'

'Just the flowery bit, idiot! Just to take the edge off of this smell.'

Sam progressed further into the shop, drawing the transphasic energy probe and using it to light the way. It wasn't much more effective than a candle flame, but it was better than nothing. He began to peer around the counter, passing the light of the wand over it.

'Look for something out of place,' he said, looking over to Alice, 'Void crystal, sigil stone, an old yo-yo covered in runes... Anything which might be an Akashic artefact.' Alice was already looking around for something along those lines, although she hadn't really considered a rune-inscribed yo-yo.

Approaching the back of the shop, Sam held the wand immediately in front of him. The pitch blackness was gently illuminated by the crystal's glow, highlighting the charcuterie. He peered closely at each item, from specialised sauces to cuts of beef, probing for anything abnormal. A pig's head appeared to be hung on the wall at about head-height, and as Sam passed the light of the probe over it the glow became a little bit brighter. Without warning, the pig head's nostrils flared, its jaw flapped, and its eyes blinked as if waking from its slumber. It shook its head, its jaw and ears flapping peculiarly, and it groaned a spine-chilling groan. Sam staggered back, his eyes wide. He kept the wand pointed firmly at it.

'Woah-oah-oah!' he exclaimed, walking backwards into a table. Alice turned to see what the fuss was about, and her mouth hung open in an expression somewhere between awe and terror. The pig head was not just reanimated, but it had begun to move forward, as if staggering on unsteady legs. As it walked into the faint light coming from the street lamps outside, it became clear why. From the neck down, the pig's head was not just a pig's head; it was a human body, standing about six foot and its clothes stained with blood. It wore a little name badge, splattered with blood, which read: "Hello! My name is Pete." The pig's dead, unseeing eyes blinked like something which didn't know how blinking worked.

'This is weird...' Sam said uneasily. He kept the probe trained on the shambling, pig-headed corpse of Pete Jones.

'Th-this is hideous!' Alice exclaimed as she took a few staggering steps backwards towards the door. The mere sight of the monstrosity sent a wave of fear and horror coursing throughout her body; the only reason she wasn't sprinting down the road at this very moment was because she'd been rooted by her fear.

'Halt right there!' Shouted a voice from somewhere behind them. 'Hands in the air, now!' Alice immediately put her hands up, turning to face whoever was shouting at them. She couldn't quite make out who it was, but from what she could see in the darkness they were wearing a police uniform. Sam simply stayed facing the creature before him, probe pointed at it in defence.

'I'd really much rather not,' he said matter-of-factly.

'I said hands in the air, now!' Screamed the voice, and the jingle of the doorbell echoed through the room as the door slowly shut.

'Officer McKenzie, is that you?' Sam asked, thinking he recognised the voice.

'Smith ordered me to keep an eye on you. I followed you here, "detective." I knew something was off... What are you doing h-' The voice of Officer McKenzie cut off mid-sentence as he stumbled over his words. The sight of the pig-headed man had caught him off-guard. 'What the hell is that thing?!'

You have come too far, spoke the pig's head, its mouth flapping awkwardly. It appeared to be speaking, but the voice which spoke to them was deep and reverberating, echoing around in their minds. It continued to limp its way forward.

'I don't exactly know,' Sam said in response to Officer McKenzie, keeping his eyes trained on the thing which had at one point been Pete Jones. 'What are you?' He asked, trying to maintain his composure while the shambling pig-man corpse marched towards him with undead intent.

'I am beyond your comprehension,' came the pig-man's response.

'Try me,' Sam said, standing straight as he challenged the creature, 'you're not my first being of inexplicable horror.' It stopped advancing and stood, swaying uncertainly.

'I transcend your very understanding, mortal. I exist in a world far beyond your own,' it spoke, its jaw flapping peculiarly like an amateur ventriloquist's dummy.

'Like the Void?' Alice asked, swallowing her fear and lowering her arms. She figured that with a demonic pig-man in front of them, Officer McKenzie was not likely to be interested in herself or Sam any more. She took a tentative step forward. The undead pig head swung unnaturally, turning to face her.

'I can sense your mind, fumbling in ignorance. There is a plane of existence so far beyond your understanding that you cannot even begin to imagine it.' Alice felt the words swim around her brain, and her blood ran cold. She could feel the malevolence of whatever this was emanating from it, filling the room and enveloping everyone in it. As she stared into its dead eyes, she felt a wave of terror wash over her again, a fear so deep her stomach began to churn. The more she locked eyes with it, the more she was overcome with the vile reality which stood before her. For a brief moment, she thought it

took pleasure in her fear.

Suddenly, two loud gunshots rung through the air. Immediately dropping to the floor, Alice took cover behind a table. She could barely hear anything over the ringing in her ears. She looked up and could see Officer McKenzie standing there, his gun pointed out directly in front of him, and two bloodied bullet holes in the chest of Pete Jones's apron. Another shot was fired, and another, but still the unearthly creature stood resiliently, seemingly unharmed by the bullets.

Officer McKenzie's eyes widened. 'Oh fu-' he slowly mouthed to himself.

'Your efforts are futile,' the voice echoed in their minds, clearly and unhindered by the deafening ringing from the gunshots, *'you only damage the vessel, you can not harm me.'* Officer McKenzie swayed uneasily as the voice overwhelmed him and he promptly collapsed to the ground, unconscious.

'You're not even really here, then,' Sam said, ignoring the police officer who'd just fallen to the floor, 'you're just using that abomination of taxidermy as a conduit.'

'This shell is merely a vehicle for my being,' intoned the voice in response.

'So this is just an avatar for your consciousness? A connection from your realm to ours. A connection that can be broken.' He kept the probe pointed at the pig-man, and the crystal glowed and pulsed with energy.

'Your words are as meaningless as your existence,

human. *You know not the magnitude of what you face,'* it said, and the pig-man took an unsteady step forward, its arms raising slowly. There was a sudden burst of light from the end of Sam's wand, and almost instantly the pig-man's body crumpled and fell to the floor, like a puppet with its strings cut.

Sam breathed a sigh of relief, and turned to Alice, who was now struggling back on to her feet. 'I severed the link, it's g-'

'You rudimentary creatures of blood and bone,' intoned that same deep and dark voice, interrupting Sam and seemingly reverberating throughout the room, *'you are incapable of understanding. I am bound to your realm by more than the mere physical. You cannot even begin to grasp the nature of my existence.'* The pig-man body lay motionless at Sam's feet. Its jaw did not flap and its eyes did not blink, yet the voice still bellowed in their minds. Alice felt a shiver run throughout her body, and judging by the look on Sam's face he had felt it too. He tightened his grip around the transphasic energy probe.

'Tell us then,' Sam spoke, 'tell us who we're facing.' There was a sinister chuckle in the darkness, a noise which sounded unlike any earthly laugh, but no answer came. 'Are you responsible for the deaths of these people? Is this your doing? The Grimditch Butcher?'

'That is how your sensationalist tabloids refer to me,' the voice sounded almost amused by this, *'a name to give form to their darkest fear. Death. An inevitability of all physical life, your kind so easily succumb to entropy,*

and yet you try to escape it. I merely expedited the end of their mortal journey. Fitting that you should come to face me here, in a butcher's shop. But that is not what I am.'

'So what should I call you?' Sam asked, but it was more of a demand than a question.

'Fallen Angel. Dark God. Demon. I have been given many names and titles across the millennia, but in the end, what you choose to call me is irrelevant. I simply am.'

'But why?' Sam addressed the room, attempting to confront the disembodied voice, 'why did you murder those people?'

There was a momentary pause before the voice spoke again. *'Because I desired it,'* came the reply.

'Really?!' Sam exclaimed incredulously. 'Just because you wanted to?'

'They were toying with powers beyond their ken. Their clumsy, primitive attempts to harness the power they held in their hands summoned me to this realm. They offered me each a drop of their blood as tribute, but I am not so easily satiated. I exacted payment with their life's blood.'

'And what gives you that right? What makes you think that you can just take human lives at your will?' Sam spoke sternly. His eyes were fixed into a solid glare, and his jaw was clenched. It was the first time Alice had really seen him burning with anger.

'You humans consider yourselves superior to the other species of your world. You claim to have the right to take the body of an animal and do with it as you please because you are superior. So too do I.'

Alice took a step forward and clenched her

fists. She spoke into the darkness of the room, addressing their invisible tormentor. 'That's different,' she started to say, and Sam gestured desperately for her to stop, but she continued regardless, 'killing a human is a lot different than killing an animal. We use animals for food, you can't do that to a person.'

Sam stared at Alice, the glare still firmly fixed on his face. The dark voice chuckled again, and Alice froze on the spot. Her body started to feel numb, and her stomach continued to churn unpleasantly. She felt as if every fibre of her being was squirming in the presence of this shapeless horror.

'And why not, young Alice Carroll? Humans consider animals lesser than themselves, only because your kind deem them to be so. Just as my kind deem you to be lesser than us. I feasted on the essence of those men, as you might feast on the flesh of an animal. And with each life I claim, with every drop of blood squeezed from their hearts, my power grows.'

'What she means,' Sam interrupted, standing directly in front of her. As he did so, she could feel the entity's nauseating focus shifting away from her. 'What she means is that human beings have a greater capacity for intelligence than the animals of this world who are not quite as cognitively developed.'

'Is that not just a matter of perspective? As a man deems himself more intelligent than a pig, would a pig not consider itself more intelligent than a worm?'

Sam paused and thought about this. There was

a certain logic to this entity's twisted reasoning, even if it was hardly justification for its actions.

'Our knowledge of the universe is greater than yours. We are not bound to a single plane of existence by such flawed vessels of flesh and bone as you are. Your kind are born into this world, you wither and die. We have no beginning. We have no end. We are infinite and eternal. Compared to us, you are nothing. We are superior.'

'It's funny,' Sam said, although by the tone of his voice he found nothing funny about it, 'that for such a superior being, so far beyond my comprehension, that you lack an evolved sense of morality. You see this Universe as a playground, its inhabitants only for your twisted amusement.'

'The forces of this Universe bend to my will. You do not yet understand your place in the vastness of eternity, mortal.' The voice was cold and dispassionate, and the butcher's shop seemed to shake with its words. Jars of condiments rattled on the shelves before falling to the floor and smashing.

'And you call that superior reasoning? A truly superior being would not think it its place to toy with lesser beings, it would see its responsibility to help make this Universe a better place; to help others, not terrorise them!'

'You are vermin. Bacteria. We will cleanse this plane of your existence.' The voice no longer sounded so measured. It spoke with wrathful intent.

'Do you know what I think of you? I don't think you're so superior at all. You talk big, but I think you're overcompensating. You're just a parasite, leeching off of the life force of other beings. A parasite with delusions of grandeur! That's why the sigils were cast in the bodies. Without feeding on their lives, your power in this realm would fade.' Sam was now shouting his words at the butcher's shop ceiling.

'You only delay the inevitable. I am the herald of your destruction.'

In the darkness, unseen things began to move and shuffle, unearthly noises calling out from the black. Alice glanced around nervously as the noises drew nearer and nearer, and Sam peered into the darkness to see what was coming. He swept the probe across the room, and the crystal's glow illuminated things he would have rather not have seen. Shambling corpses marauded from the dark corners of the butcher's shop, the cut-up and hollowed-out pig bodies one normally sees hanging from the ceiling or in the window of a butcher's were making their way across the floor. Their short had-been-limbs dragged the carcasses forward.

'You are in my domain. You creatures, so small. So inferior. You thrive in the light of day and hide away from the dark, clinging to your insignificant rock, adrift in the cosmic void. Before the Universe there was only the Void, and when the last sun dies out only Darkness will remain.'

With a sudden burst of unnatural energy, one of the bodies launched itself at Alice, knocking her to the floor. She yelped, struggling beneath the weight of the carcass, trying to push it off of her, but it had her pinned down. She kicked at it, but still it lay on top of her, writhing around and exuding the foul stench of decaying meat. A bolt of purple energy shot across the room, hitting the pig carcass and throwing it off of her. She turned to see what had happened and saw Sam standing just off to the side, the transphasic energy probe pointed in her direction and a look of triumph on his face.

'I was really hoping I wouldn't miss!' He said.

You will die here. All of your kind will perish. This speck of dust you call Earth will be your tomb, and my kind shall retake our rightful place as the masters of this Universe.' The voice sounded as if it was raging against them, screaming in their minds with fury and hatred.

'Not if I can help it!' Sam shouted back, and another burst of purple energy erupted from the wand. It struck another of the carcasses, sending it flying back into the wall with an unpleasant and meaty thud.

'Confidence born of foolishness. You fight against the inevitable, Sam Hain, like dust struggling against a cosmic wind,' the voice boomed through-out the room.

Another of the pig-like husks threw itself towards Sam, and he fired another bolt of energy at it. It hit its mark a short distance from his face, throwing the body back and splitting it in half, flesh exploding and tearing from the impact.

'Alice, keep looking,' Sam instructed, glancing over to her, 'it's got to be here! We need to finish this.'

'What am I looking for?!' Alice yelled back, running from the reanimated pig bodies which were slowly trying to follow her. They may have only been crawling after her, but she felt like she was living a nightmare. She prayed she'd wake up soon and have a normal Thursday, but she knew that wouldn't happen.

'Trust your instincts, find it. Whatever it is. You'll know it when you see it.' He pointed the wand at Alice's pursuers, and a wave of energy pushed them back, but still they carried on moving forward, their stubby limbs carrying them as fast as they could crawl.

'Your efforts are futile. You cannot break the cycle.' The voice sounded almost mocking.

'Cycle? What cycle?' Sam asked, and he noticed the pig bodies slowed their advance when he asked the entity this question.

Alice made a dash for the shop counter, getting behind it and crouching down to hide from their attackers. She knew it wouldn't help – she could sense that it could see, or feel, everything in that room – but at least it made her feel a little more protected. It was then that she looked up and saw the cash register.

The cycle has continued for longer than you could possibly fathom. The pattern repeats itself time and time again. All of this has happened before, and all of this will happen again.'

'What cycle? Answer me!' Sam shouted, throwing his arms wide open as if inviting the being to take a piece of him.

'Know this as you die in vain. The time of our return is imminent. Darkness is coming. The Old Ones shall awaken from their slumber and blacken the skies of your

world. You will know your doom.'

Alice hastily tried to unlock the till, tapping numbers at random in the desperate hope she'd hit upon the right combination. Nothing happened. She looked up nervously and saw more of the reanimated meat making its way towards her. The room suddenly seemed darker than it did before, and she could barely see what she was doing. She tried to suppress her fear and attempted to focus on the right combination.

'You resist, but you will fail. The time will come, and your kind will beg to serve us!'

Sam managed to repel another of the husks with an energy burst, but the energy flowing through the crystal was waning. It sputtered with each progressive shot, and he could feel himself becoming more and more drained. He leapt up on top of one of the tables, giving himself the high ground over their attackers. 'Now would be a *really* good time for some divine inspiration, Alice!'

8. 1. 7. 2. The numbers flashed through Alice's mind, and she knew she had the answer. *Douglas's birthday, 8th of January, 1972. That must be it...* She hit the keypad, and with a triumphant *cha-ching*, the till's cash-draw flung open. There, in one of the compartments, sat a peculiar object. It appeared to be a smooth stone, perfectly ovular, with a series of unearthly symbols carved into its surface. In the centre of the stone was engraved a spiral pattern, and even though Alice knew it wasn't possible, she thought she could see the stone glowing with a black taint. As she tentatively picked up the strange object, she noticed it easily fit in the palm of her hand, and with a hopeful throw she chucked it in Sam's direction. 'Catch!'

Sam staggered as he attempted to catch the small stone, almost losing his footing and falling off of the table in the process. He only just managed to catch it, clutching it between his fingers. He held it up above his head.

'You see this?!' He cried out in triumph, waving the strange stone around, taunting the entity. 'After all that talk, all those grandiose statements, now *I* will be the one to end *you.*' His voice was tainted with a dark vengeance Alice had never heard before, and she wasn't in a hurry to ever hear it again. Sam cast the engraved stone onto the floor, and pointed his wand at it.

'You consider this a victory, mortal? You've changed nothing. You have the attention of those infinitely greater than yourselves. You will know pain.'

'That may be so, but you won't be around to see it. Give my regards to your Dark Masters. Bye-bye.' The crystal at the probe's tip began to glow violet, crackling and sparking as it charged up.

'You are arrogant. You cannot kill me. I always survive. I am eternal. My essence lives on in the bleeding hearts of men, in their sorrow and their hatred. I thrive on your darkest emotions. You can not destroy me.'

The wand erupted with a bright purple beam of energy, tearing through the air, sparking and hissing as the energy beam spiralled towards the stone and striking it with a sudden burst of violet flame. The stone shattered into countless fragments, leaving nothing more than a scorch mark and its scattered shards. The voice echoed in their minds no more.

There was a sickening thud as the reanimated animal corpses fell to the ground, and Alice breathed a sigh of relief. Sam jumped down from the table and ran over to her, throwing his arms wide and taking her in an embrace. He could feel her body trembling.

'Are you okay?' He whispered.

'I'll be all right,' she uttered through uncertain breaths. 'It was right, though, you know. That entity, it was right. You may have destroyed the artefact, but it's not gone. I could feel it. It's still out there, somewhere, filled with nothing but fury and hatred.'

Sam nodded silently. He knew it was still out there; they always were. But presently that didn't matter. What mattered now was that it was cut off from their realm, unable to return. Unable to cause more harm. And that, to him, was victory enough.

'Come on,' he eventually said, releasing her from his embrace with a firm pat on the shoulder, 'let's get out of this place.' He made his way towards the door, stepping over the still-unconscious body of Officer McKenzie, and with the cheery jingling of the little bell Sam opened the door.

'What about him?' Alice asked, pointing back to the policeman laying prone in the middle of the butcher's shop, surrounded by bits and pieces of animal flesh.

'He'll come to, sooner or later. And I don't want to be around when he does; an unconscious police officer, coming round on the floor of the butcher's shop with the two people impersonating officers of the law, who he now suspects of murder, with another dead body and no substantial evidence pointing to a real, physical, human suspect? I don't think he'd be too pleased! And suggesting that a demon from another dimension committed these murders... That's a one-way ticket to prison or a psychiatric hospital!' He stepped out into the cold night air of Grimditch and took a deep breath. He held the door open for Alice while he rummaged around in his pockets, looking for something. He pulled out a battered box, and withdrew a crumpled cigarette from the packet. Sam lit the cigarette and took a long, deep drag, exhaling a cloud of smoke into the air.

'Since when do you smoke?' Alice asked incredulously.

'Since I had a shouting match with a demon and had to fend off a selection of reanimated charcuterie. That kind of magick isn't easy, it really takes it out of you.' He took another long drag on the cigarette. 'Now come on,' he said, 'it's late. We'd better be going.'

The taxi ride back to Islington was quiet and uneventful. Sam spent the majority of the time staring out of the window, lost in thought. He turned the evidence over and over in his head, from sigils carved in human flesh to the hideous artefact and its demonic connections. And the talk of Regents in Douglas's emails, what part did they have to play in all of this? All Sam really knew was that, although whatever they'd just encountered was no longer here, this was only the beginning of something more.

Alice too had been lost in thought, although she wasn't quite as preoccupied with the sinister portents of the day. Seeing the decapitated body and severed head of Douglas Norton now seemed like a distant memory, and only now was she starting to see the strangeness of what had just befallen them. Looking back, she was overcome with horror and revulsion as images of mutilated corpses, animated porcine carcasses and the shambling pig-headed man flooded her mind. Her stomach churned with the mere memory, and she shook the images from her mind. Instead, she started to wonder what she'd done to deserve this, and exactly why she had been drawn into this man's strange and terrifying universe.

The cab stopped with a subtle jolt as it pulled up outside of Alice's house. None of the lights were on, save for the dim glow of the hallway light; presumably all of the other tenants were either still out or asleep by now. Alice bid a quick thank you to the driver, and stepped out onto the curb. Sam also stepped out onto the street with her. 'Thank you for today,' he said in a perfectly normal way, as if they'd just been out to dinner or some other normal activity, 'it's been... interesting.'

'I'm not sure that's the word I'd have used, but sure. Interesting,' she replied.

'You know what I mean,' Sam said with a

smile, but his face immediately shifted back to a serious expression. 'Listen, if you need anything, if anything happens, I-'

'I know,' Alice cut him off, 'but if I can survive the Little Butcher's Shop of Horrors, I'm sure I'll be just fine in my own home. Thank you, though.'

'You're starting to wake up and see the world for how it really is, Alice. You're experiencing things in a way many people can't even begin to imagine. But some of these things really don't like people being aware of them...'

'Well thank you so much for that,' Alice said sarcastically, 'it's not like I was planning on getting any sleep tonight or anything!'

'Just be mindful,' Sam said, 'you know how to reach me. Have a good night.' With that, he got back into the taxi.'

'Good night,' Alice reciprocated, and she waved as the taxi drove off down the road, around the corner and into the night. She opened the door to the house, made her way up the stairs and entered the first door on the right. She headed straight for bed, where she dreamed dreams of shapeless beings lurking in the shadows, and of the dazzling white light from which they were hiding.

The following day, Alice tried to put the thoughts of the events of Grimditch out of her mind. She was surprised she wasn't quite as haunted by the image of corpses as she thought she would be, but still she felt a lingering sense of uneasiness. Try as she might to forget, flashes would dance across her mind's eye, and she'd remember with haunting clarity the words the disembodied voice had spoken. And that ever present phrase which warned that darkness was coming. She couldn't easily forget, and what she once called reality now seemed to be a desperate distraction from the actual real world.

That Friday evening, Alice was sat watching the television, eating dinner. She was experimenting with a vegetarian burger and, much to her surprise, it didn't taste like cardboard. In fact, she thought, she could get used to it. The lock in the front door clicked as a key turned in it, and Rachel walked in.

'I'm back,' she announced with a weary but almost-triumphant voice, dropping her bag on the floor with a dead thud.

'Hey, how was it?' Alice asked, craning around to see Rachel.

'Ugh, don't ask. I'd rather forget the whole thing,' she said, and Alice felt similarly about her experience. 'So, what's new? Anything interesting happen while I was away?'

'I'm vegetarian now,' was Alice's simple response, and she lifted the not-cardboard-y veggie burger up as proof. 'Cup of tea?' She asked, putting her plate down and standing up to make her way out into the kitchen.

'That'd be wonderful,' Rachel replied, following her. 'So what's this about vegetarianism?'

'*Police have released the image of a man they suspect to be involved in the recent Grimditch murders,*' the newsreader on the television announced to the now empty living room. '*Reports indicate that this man may be guilty of concealing vital evidence and perverting the course of justice, as he was sighted at key locations during the investigation and masquerading as a police officer.*' A photo-fit image of a man who looked not entirely unlike Sam Hain appeared on the screen. '*The Metropolitan Police warns that this man, who goes by the name of Arthur Doyle, may be dangerous and must be approached with caution. Now here's Tom with the weather.*'

'*Forget about that early Springtime we were promised, Sally,*' said Tom with the Weather, surrounded by cartoon clouds with sad faces, '*it looks like we're not out of the dark yet.*'

About the Author

Bron James is an author of science fiction, fantasy and magical realism. He was born with a silver pen in his mouth and has been making up stories for as long as he can remember. His professional début work of fiction, the first instalment of the *Sam Hain* series of novellas, was first published in 2013.

Born and raised in the south of England, Bron presently lives in London where he writes stories, drinks tea, and dreams improbable dreams.

~

www.bronjames.co.uk

MORE TITLES IN THE *SAM HAIN* SERIES

<u>Volume I</u>

All Hallows' Eve
A Night in Knightsbridge
The Grimditch Butcher
The Regents
The Eye of the Oracle
Convergence

~

www.samhainscasebook.co.uk

Printed in Great Britain
by Amazon